Kid's Zombie Adventure Series - Powers of the Unknown

Author : Berry Wood

Story Inspiration: Tahara & Hasani Woodberry

(The Best Kid's EVER)

Website : http://kidszombieadventures.com/

AMANDA

KAYDEN

MICHAEL

SAMMY

Chapter 1. Test Run

As Amanda made her way over the path that snaked its way along the edge of the lake, she looked at the zombies around her. Glancing over her shoulder, she saw Kayden and the others making their way over the hillside and quickly fading out of sight.

"Good, they should be safe" she muttered to herself as she ran on, focusing on the task at hand and what she had to do. "Time to get serious!"

A few snarls from behind her served as a stark reminder that there were zombies following her- about 20 altogether in fact. That was a few more than she had anticipated, but she was pretty sure her plan would still work out fine. Quickening her pace, Amanda slid the pack off her back and pulled out the length of rope she had placed in there before heading out.

"Alright you zombies! Come and get me!' she called to the monsters behind her as she changed her course, leaving the lake and heading up into the woods.

The zombies followed after her as she began weaving her way in and out through the trees. Amanda scanned the trees on the horizon as she slowed her pace and set her eyes on a tall straight pine tree right ahead of her. Letting the zombies get as close to her as she dared, she ran right for the tree, her path not wavering at all. When she was right in front of the tree, she planted her foot on the trunk of the tree and with her momentum, ran up the trunk of the tree, the zombies right behind her.

Like a monkey, Amanda ran almost ten feet up the trunk of the tree before pushing off and flipping backwards, landing back on the ground. The zombies that had been following her ran headlong into the tree, ending up in a dazed pile at the base of the tree. Quickly, Amanda grabbed the rope and ran around the tree a few times, tying the zombies snuggly to the tree. Smirking slightly, she looked at the five zombies that now lay in a tangled heap.

Celebrating would have to wait though as she still had over a dozen zombies coming up the hillside to deal with.

****

Sammy stood and watched Amanda head down the shoreline, cutting right through the middle of the zombies. She flew past them so quickly there was no chance of them catching her, but as expected, they started to shamble after her.

"She sure has gotten fast!" he muttered as he turned to help Michael and Kayden with the packs and supplies that sat on the deck of the boat.

"That is what her gift from the water seems to be" Michael said as they jumped off the deck and headed up the shoreline.

"Wish I had gotten something special from the water..."
Sammy said as they headed up the first small hillside that rose up ahead of them.

Kayden was about to answer but an odd groan cut him off. Staggering to a stop, the three friends looked over and saw a small group of about ten zombies heading their way.

"Oh of course... that's just wonderful!" Sammy said sarcastically as he swallowed hard.

"Come on, we have to keep going" Kayden said. "Amanda's got a lot more zombies than this to deal with. We can take care of these guys for her!"

"Here, take these" Michael said, tossing something to Sammy and Kayden. Two long walking sticks fell into their hands.

"I found them on the boat right before we got off. Figured they might be good for warding off the zombies. You two head on up towards the meeting place, I'll follow."

"Michael, what are you...."

"Kayden, just do it! I'm going to try and lay some traps for the zombies to slow them down as they come after us."

By now the zombies were heading towards them at a quick pace. With a nod Kayden and Sammy took off, continuing down the trail. One of the zombies followed after them but the other kept coming right for Michael.

"Alright, let's see what you got!"

With that, Michael faced the oncoming zombies and reached back into his pack and pulled out a small hand net used for fishing. With a quick flick of the wrist, he threw the net towards the zombies and it hit one of them in the face. As it staggered trying to free itself, the zombie knocked a few others down with it, all of them getting caught up in the net. Smiling slightly to himself, Michael took off after Sammy and Kayden, the remaining few zombies shambling off after him.

Sammy ran along after Kayden as they weaved in and out among the trees, trying to lose the three zombies that were now on their tail. Kayden scanned the area, looking for something that might help them and gave a happy shout when he saw the tree up ahead.

"Sammy! Head for that tree" he said as he pointed ahead of them. "When we get there, climb up into one of the lower branches, but make sure you are out of the zombie's reach."

"Ok, but what are you going to?"

"You'll see" Kayden said with an almost delightful smirk on his face.

Within moments they were at the tree and Sammy was climbing up into the branches. Kayden stood on the ground, behind one of the low growing branches that was only a few feet off the ground. Grabbing hold of the branch, which was a pretty big branch actually, Kayden started to pull it back as the Zombies approached.

From his perch up in the tree, Sammy saw the zombies getting closer and it didn't look like Kayden was ready yet. So he started looking around for the walking stick he had laying on the branch beside him, but when he went to grab it, his fingers bumped it, causing it to slide off the branch and fall to the ground. By some miracle though, the walking stick fell on a nearby zombie, hitting it in the head, and knocking it out cold.

"Thanks Sammy! Good hit!" Kayden shouted as he finished pulling the branch back.

"Oh, ummm... don't mention it!" Sammy called back with a sheepish grin on his face.

"Alright you ugly things... eat tree branch!" Kayden exclaimed as the remaining zombies staggered closer, so close one of them almost touched him.

With a sudden swooshing sound, the tree branch snapped back, hitting the zombies and sending them flying cross the small clearing and smacking into another tree.

"Alright Sammy, let's go!"

Sammy nodded and scampered down, picked up his walking stick and followed after Kayden as they made their way to the meeting place to wait for the others.

Chapter 2. Powers Realized

After dealing with the first few zombies, Amanda ran further into the thickest part of the wooded area, weaving in and out between the trees as the zombies trailed behind her. With the parkour moves of a pro, she jumped and zipped her way around the trees, sending zombies crashing into trees and each other with every move. After a few minutes she started to head back towards the shore and the boat, taking a different path than before so as not to regain the attention of the zombies she had already managed to shake off her trail.

She dealt with the last zombie by scrambling up a tree and waiting for the zombie to stagger over. As the zombie aimlessly circled the tree, trying to find a way to get at her, Amanda jumped from her perch and landed safely on one of the branches of the nearby tree and scampered down to safety. With the zombies gone she allowed herself to slow down slightly as she made her towards the meeting point, praying that her friends had made it away safely.

****

Michael kept following Sammy and Kayden, stopping every now and then to lay a trap for the zombies that were tailing them. Using some of the rope from the boat, he laid a few rabbit snare traps for the zombies as well as some trip lines. With any luck, they would thin out the number of the undead beasties that were following them and would hopefully buy them a little more time to get away.

As he finished stretching out the last trip line, Michael stood and turned quickly as he heard a snap of a twig behind him. He stared into the trees, but couldn't see anything. Something was out there, but he didn't want to wait around to find out what it was or how big it was. Grabbing his pack, he reached in and took out a few of the remaining glow sticks and activated them. As he ran, he threw the glowing sticks along his path, hoping that in the setting sun and dimming light they would distract the zombies and get them off their trail.

As Michael ran on, his thoughts were on Amanda and he hoped that she was alright and that she was either already at the meeting spot waiting for them or that she was not too far behind them. He pushed the fear from his mind and quickened his pace, wanting to get to the others as soon as possible.

****

Kayden and Sammy had an easy go of it after shaking the few zombies that were following them. Nothing else was in the area, no birds, no animals.... and no Michael or Amanda either. Sammy glanced over at Kayden nervously as they ran up to the tree at the top of the hill and stood there alone.

"Kayden, where are...'

"They will be here! I know it. They will be here soon" he said firmly as he scanned the wooded area they had just come from. Michael shouldn't have been too far behind them and Amanda should have made it there by now too.

The two friends stood there waiting, when suddenly there was movement at the edge of the woods near the foot of the hill. They held their breath, not knowing whether to expect their friends or more zombies. The setting sun cast a strange eerie light on the trees as they waited. The rustling grew louder and then suddenly from out of the trees stumbled Michel, walking stick still in hand. Glancing over his shoulder he gave a slight sigh of relief as he scurried up the hill alone.

"Michael!" exclaimed Sammy happily.

"Great to see that you made it" Kayden said as he and Sammy hugged Michael.

"That... was tricky" Michael huffed as he set his pack down and sat down, leaning against the tree. "Where's Amanda?"

"She hasn't made it here yet."

Michael gave Sammy a concerned look as Kayden cleared his throat softly.

"I'm sure she is fine, Michael. She will probably be here any minute now."

Michael nodded and nervously pulled at a tuft of grass beside him as he stared down the hill towards to the woods. After a few minutes there was a rustling from the woods and the friends all turned to look. Amanda ran out from in between the trees, her head craned to look behind her as a zombie followed right behind her.

"Amanda!" they all called as they jumped to their feet.

Sammy scrambled up a bit too quickly and tripped over his own feet and started tumbling head over heels down the hillside towards Amanda and the zombie. He landed with a thud face first in the dirt and let out a groan as he started to push himself up.

Amanda kept running towards him, the zombie right behind her. Sammy and Amanda locked eyes for a split second as Kayden and Michael stood on the hill shouting and yelling. As Sammy pushed himself up onto his hands and knees and tried to stand, Amanda ran up to him and jumped, her feet landing on Sammy's back as she ran over his back for a few steps and then kicked off. As she somersaulted through the air, Sammy fell back to the ground with a groan and Amanda landed on the ground, giving a quick kick as she landed, sending the Zombie flying back into the woods.

"Sammy are you ok?" Amanda asked as she helped him back to his feet.

"Yeah... yeah I'm fine. You?"

"Yeah... let's go. He won't be gone for long."

Together they ran up the hill and joined Kayden and Michael. There was not much time for celebrating or welcoming. They all knew they had to keep going because even though they had bought themselves some time, the zombies would soon be after them again.

"So where we heading now?" Michael asked as pulled out the map and opened it.

Chapter 3. Tales of Survival

"Which way is North?" Kayden asked as he looked at the map.

"That way" Michael pointed out away from them, down the hillside and towards the distant mountain range.

"According to the map, we need to head Northeast then and we will hit the closest city. Doesn't look like it is too far away on the map... we might actually be able to reach it in the next hour or so."

"So in other words right when it will be getting dark."

Kayden looked at Amanda and gave her a look.

"It is better than staying out here in the middle of no where all night. If we can reach the city we can at least find someplace to get shelter for the night" Kayden said, trying to sound convinced himself.

"Or it could be overrun with zombies" Sammy muttered under his breath.

"Come on. We got to keep moving" Kayden urged as they stood and started off down the other side of the hill, towards their destination. The sun was sinking low in the sky and everything was cast in the faint light and long shadows of sunset.

****

About an hour later, the four friends stood outside the city limits. Before them stretched the bridge that crossed over the Switchback River and lead into the city. Under the bridge in the light of the now rising moon, were the silhouetted forms of zombies, wading through the waist high water. Steep banks were keeping a lot of them trapped in the water as most simply slid back down the banks when they tried to climb back out. However, there were a few standing on the bridge, wandering around aimlessly up and down the bridge and roadway leading into the city.

"Figures doesn't it?" muttered Sammy as he scanned the area. "We finally get to the city and its full of zombies."

"We don't know how bad it is inside. Most of them might be trapped out here" Amanda said, trying to sound optimistic.

"So how are we going to get in? That's the bigger question right now" Michael said as he scratched his head and thought.

"I'd say we need to split up."

"I agree with Kayden" Michael said. "We stand too much of a chance of attracting the zombies if we all try to get past them at the same time. One on one we can slip by easier."

Everyone nodded in agreement. Even though no one really liked the idea of facing the zombies on their own, there was no denying the truth of what Michael was saying.

"I'll go first" Kayden said as he crouched down and started drawing a picture of the bridge in the sand at their feet. "Sammy, you come after me. It looks like the zombies are keeping on a fairly steady path so just watch where they are going and avoid them as much as possible by hiding behind the crates and cars that are on the bridge as you come up."

"I'll follow after Sammy" Amanda chimed in.

"And I'll be last so I can try to distract any zombies that try to come after you all" Michael said as he held up a few of his homemade traps and snares.

"Alright then, let's do this!" Kayden said as he stood and turned to face the bridge.

After a few moments of preparation, they were ready and Kayden was already making his way over the bridge. He started off at a run and then kicked off and jumped up onto a small pile of wood pallets that lay on the bridge. From there he jumped again and climbed up onto a stack of crates. There was a wide gap between his perch and the next stack of crates he needed to get too, and several zombies wandered around on the ground between them. Glancing around, Kayden grabbed a long metal pole that was propped up against his crate tower. Stretching out as far as he could he planted the pole in the broken chunks of asphalt and then gave a great shove as he swung himself off the crates, using the pole to swing over the heads of the zombies and landed on the other side safely. He quickly jumped down off the crates and sprinted the short distance over the open section of the bridge and ran up to an abandoned car that sat at the end of the bridge by the entrance to the town. He gave the signal that he had made it and it was Sammy's turn to make the trip across the bridge.

Sammy swallowed hard as he tried to calm the nervous shaking of his knees. He crept to the edge of the bridge and gave a glance behind him. Amanda and Michael nodded and taking a deep breath, he started to run towards a pile of rubble nearby. He waited behind it for a moment, then poked his head out to check for any nearby zombies. When the coast was clear he made the short sprint to the pile of crates Kayden had used. Sammy leaned back against the boxes as he waited for the nearby zombie to wander off and then he snuck to the abandoned car nearby. Sammy continued on creeping and hiding as he made his way across the bridge and soon joined Kayden on the other side. The signal was given again and it was Amanda's turn.

As Amanda grabbed her pack and slung it over her shoulders, she started towards the bridge. However, she took a different path than the others. Instead of heading towards the roadway, she worked her way down the embankment in one of the few spots that was free of zombies. With an agile leap, she grabbed onto the metal beams under the bridge and started making her way across the bridge, swinging along the bottom of the bridge, her feet dangling above the heads of the zombies wandering around in the water below. About half way across, she reached an area where the bridge has partially collapsed in that spot. Pulling herself up onto the beams, she stood and after gaining her balance, jumped across the gap. As she landed, she grabbed onto the beams on the other side and continued on her way. When she reached the other side, she climbed up through the supports, poking her head out through a hole in the road way just a little ways away from Kayden and Sammy. She pulled herself up and scrambled over to them, signaling to Michael that it was his turn.

Adjusting the pack on his back, Michael started walking out onto the bridge. In his hand was the last two glow sticks from the camp. Cracking them open he started waving them around to get the zombie's attention. As the creatures started towards him he threw the sticks, one to the left and the other to the right and climbed up on the top of one of the stacks of crates. As the zombies staggered after the glow sticks, Michael quickly ran between the separating groups and slid to a stop under one of the abandoned cars. Reaching into his pocket, he grabbed several of the super bouncy strobe light balls he had found in the supply closet at the camp before they left. Watching the zombies shuffle by from his hiding place, Michael waited for the right moment then started tossing the balls out, letting them bounce around across the broken surface of the bridge. The zombies shambled after them, moaning and reaching for the flashing orbs. With that distraction, Michael made the final sprint across the bridge, jumping over the car the others were hiding behind and landed beside them with a soft pant.

"Well that was exciting" Michael said with a slight laugh.

"Great job team. Come on let's go!"

Kayden stood and the others followed as they slipped into the city through the shadows. The full moon overhead cast soft white beams of light into the city and made it easy for the friends to find their way through the streets and alleyways without the risk of lights or a fire. Everything looked eerily empty in the moonlight and a cool chilling breeze blew through the dark and silent streets as the friends made their way deeper into the city.

Chapter 4. A Surprising Discovery

Making their way through the city by the light of the moon, the four friends soon found that the place was a bit more empty than they had anticipated. Aside from the few zombies they could see shuffling by, there seemed to be nothing else moving in the city.

"Where is everyone?" Sammy asked as they stopped for a breather and crouched down behind an old worn out looking truck. "This is a pretty big city. There should be people all over the place!"

"They are either hiding, already left the city, or been turned into zombies already" Amanda said a slight shiver in her voice.

"Well let's hope it's that first one" Michael muttered as he shook his empty canteen. "We really need to stock up on supplies!"

"Hiding around out here is not going to help us any" Kayden said standing to his feet. "We need to find some shelter for the night. We can start checking out the city in the morning."

"One of the buildings is going to probably be our best bet" Sammy said pointing to the nearby gas station. "It will also likely have food in there too."

"Great idea, Sammy" Amanda said with a smile. "We can get a place to sleep, stay out of the storm that seems to be brewing, and maybe find a bite to eat."

It didn't take too long before they were inside the gas station and scouting out the place. After a quick check to see if there were any zombies inside, they settled on one of the back office rooms as the best place to settle down for the night. Michael set up a quick trip wire alarm to alert them if any zombies came down the hallway. Amanda found some pillows and blankets in one of the closets and soon they were settling in for the night.

"Tomorrow we scout out the place and see what supplies we can find" Kayden said as they drifted off to sleep.

"And then we search the town to see what else and who else we can find" Michael added as he yawned and felt his eyes grow heavy.

"I wonder if there is anyone left here in the city" Amanda mused as she started to drift off to sleep. "What do you think, Sammy?"

The only sound that came from Sammy was a soft snore. The friends chuckled softly and then settled down for the night, the distant moans of the zombies seeming for the first time to be a distant threat. Soft rain began to fall, rattling lightly against the metal roof over their heads and soon they were sleeping as comfortably as they had in some time.

****

With the first rays of light in the morning, the four friends were up and exploring the gas station and the surrounding area. Between the food that was still left and the supplies they found in a back closet, they were able to restock their food supply and get some other great resources.

Kayden and Michael had their packs stuffed full with food and supplies and securely strapped on as they started on their way. As they headed for the front door of the gas station, Kayden poked his head outside and glanced around before ducking back in.

"There are zombies in the city still. I see at least three of them over by the gas pumps. Those are the only ones I can see right now... but there may be others around, so be careful."

Quietly the four friends crept out and made their way around to the back of the gas station. The zombies paid them little attention and they were able to get past them with no trouble at all. Putting his finger to his lips to keep them quiet, Kayden motioned towards the other side of the street where a large sporting goods store stood. With a knowing nod and smile they followed, weaving this way in and out among the abandoned cars and debris that littered the streets.

"We have to stop in here" Michael whispered as they stood outside the doors to the large sports store.

"I agree" Kayden whispered as he walked up and pulled open the automatic doors that no longer worked since the city seemed to be without electricity.

Large skylights in the roof of the complex lit everything up nicely in the bright morning sun and the friends stood there staring in amazement at the sheer size of the place. Hunting supplies, camping equipment, tools, clothes, and much more filled the shelves and walls. It looked like it had been picked over some and there were some overturned shelves and tables but the majority of the place seemed to be just as it should have been on any day it was open.

"Jackpot!" Kayden said as he broke into a smile and started towards the camping equipment and supplies.

Sammy and Amanda headed for the sports section and Michael stared at the large selection of tools and equipment. As they wandered along the rows of shelves and tables of goods, there was so much to look at that their small packs were soon at maximum capacity.

"I think it's time for an upgrade" Kayden said as he slipped off his pack and picked up a big camping backpack off the shelf. Grabbing some of the camping supplies off the shelf nearby he began filling the pack. "Might as well make use of my strength. If I can carry it we might as well have it."

Michael looked over at him from across the aisle and nodded and slipped his own pack off and added in some things he had found- more rope, a fishing net, another handful of glow sticks, and other odds and ends.

A long whistle caught everyone's attention as Amanda stood in the middle of one of the aisle and stared, mouth open in wonder. Before her lay the entire hunting department. Several cross bows lay on the shelf, some paint guns were still sitting on the table, and many other things that could be used to fight the zombies were there for the taking.

"We struck gold with this place" Sammy said as he walked up to the others, his arms full of things like a tarp, some rope, flashlights and batteries, a compass, lantern, and a tinder box.

"We are going to have to sort through all this stuff" Michael said as he looked over the pile of things they all had gathered. "I'm not sure if we are going to be able to carry it all."

The others nodded in agreement and began sorting things into different piles to get everything organized. Then suddenly, a shrill cry tore through the sports center. Sammy jumped and dropped the compass he had been holding. Amanda gave a little yelp of surprise as the others jumped to their feet.

"What... what was that?"

"It... it almost sounded...." Michael got interrupted as the cry was heard again, louder and closer now.

"That was human!" Amanda exclaimed. "It came from outside!"

"Someone's out there!" cried Kayden as he ran towards the front of the store, the others following close behind trying to see who, or what, was outside.

TO BE CONTINUED.......

http://kidszombieadventures.com/

COLORING BOOK PAGES

Create your own zombie horde
with these fun coloring pages-
inspired from the story!

Have fun and thanks for reading!

http://kidszombieadventures.com/

AMANDA

AMANDA

KAYDEN

KAYDEN

MICHAEL

MICHAEL

SAMMY

SAMMY

http://kidszombieadventures.com/

www.ingramcontent.com/pod-product-compliance
Lightning Source LLC
Chambersburg PA
CBHW041133170626
46815CB00009B/347